Surprise! Snow Day!

by Courtney Baker
Illustrated by Patti Goodnow

Hello Reader! — Level 1

SCHOLASTIC INC.

New York   Toronto   London   Auckland   Sydney
Mexico City   New Delhi   Hong Kong   Buenos Aires

Winter is here.
I press my face against the glass.
I peek outside and see a gray sky.

I put on my jacket, scarf, hat, and mittens.
Then I step outside and look around.

The trees are bare.
Leaves are on the ground.

Everything is quiet.

The wind blows cold
and burns my cheeks.

I walk along in a fluffy jacket.
I wiggle my fingers in my mittens.

I turn around and what a surprise!
Something cold and small brushes by.

Just to be sure, I look up to the sky
and see small white flakes falling dow

"It's snowing! It's snowing!" I shout.
The ground is turning white.
Snowflakes melt in my hand
and on my face.

Soon, I can make snow angels
on the ground.

I take giant steps and turn around.
I see my footsteps far behind.

I think of all the games I can play!

I can make a snowman with raisin eyes
and a carrot nose.

I can make an igloo with a tunnel door.

I play and play until I start to feel col
I sniffle a little and rub my nose.

Mommy comes outside and says,
"It's time to come in."

Inside, I cover myself
with a warm, fuzzy blanket.

I watch the snow fall outside.

Mommy gives me hot cocoa and a hu
I tell her all about my great snow day.

I hurry to bed and fall asleep.

I dream of all the snow
that will be waiting for me!